Big Dog Little Dog

visit the Moon

Selina Young

BLue Bananas

"☆ for Louie and Tail
the real
Big Dog and
Little Dog ☆"

Big Dog and Little Dog visit the Moon

Selina Young

First published in Great Britain 1996
by Egmont Books Ltd,
239 Kensington High St, London W8 6SA
Published in hardback by Heinemann Library,
a division of Reed Educational and Professional Publishing Ltd
by arrangement with Egmont Books Ltd.
Text copyright © Selina Young 1996
Illustrations copyright © Selina Young 1996
The author and illustrator have asserted their moral rights
Paperback ISBN 1 4052 0139 8
Hardback ISBN 0 4349 75457 9
10
A CIP catalogue record for this title is available from the British Library.
Printed and bound in the U.A.E.

One night, when Big Dog and Little Dog were going home, they saw the moon in the sky. He was big and yellow, but he looked sad. 'Poor Moon,' said Little Dog.

Let's cheer Moon up.

Yes, let's go and see him.

Big Dog and Little Dog went home

and made plans to build a rocket.

They would fly to the moon.

Big Dog did lots of drawings.

Little Dog coloured them in.

They made a list.

Big Dog took all the money from their

Piggy Bank. He gave it to Little Dog.

Little Dog went shopping and bought

the things they needed.

When Little Dog got back,
Big Dog checked the shopping.
There was: cardboard, string,
sticky tape, wallpaper paste,
elastic bands, plasticine
and paint.

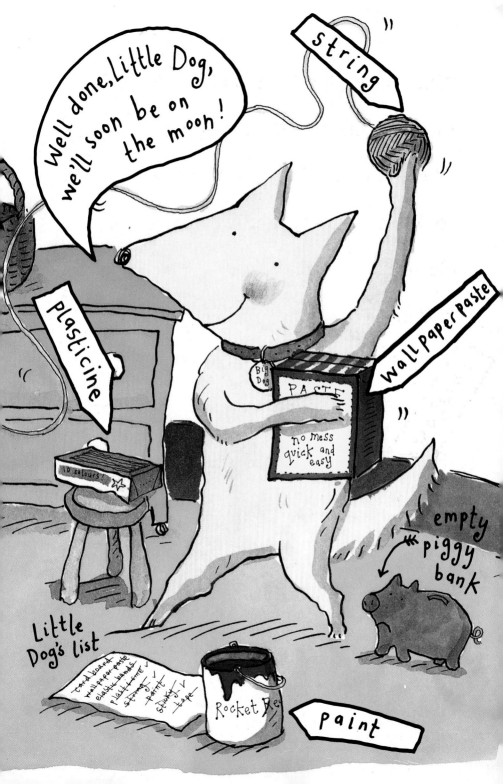

Big Dog cut out cardboard shapes.

Little Dog stuck them together

with sticky tape.

Big Dog made important

rocket bits out of plasticine.

Little Dog tied them on with string.

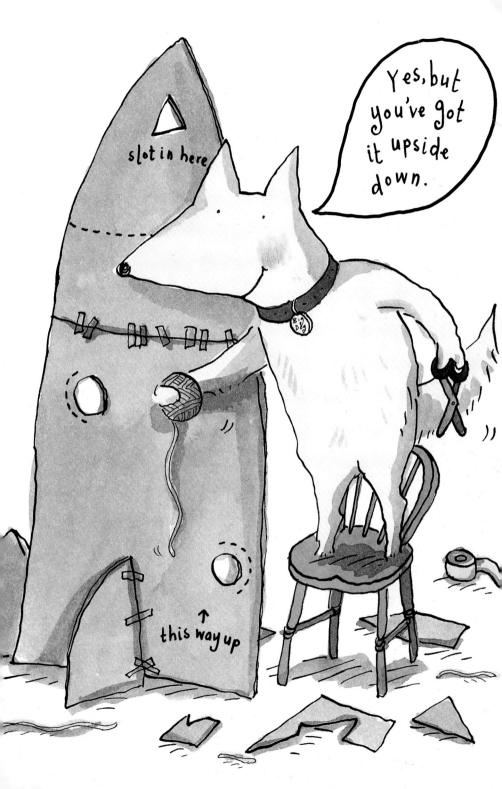

Little Dog tore up some newspaper.

Big Dog mixed some wallpaper paste.

Then they stuck the newspaper all over

the cardboard and plasticine rocket.

They were tired after all their

cutting and sticking and pasting.

So they went to bed.

The moon shone outside the bedroom
window. He glowed over the
house in a gloomy way.
He didn't know Big
Dog and Little Dog
were planning to
visit him and
cheer him
up.

Wispy grey clouds hung round his eyes.

In the morning, Big Dog and Little Dog woke early. They had a big breakfast.

Then they went to look at the rocket.

During the night the newspaper and paste had set hard. A big solid rocket stood on the carpet.

Little Dog fetched the paint.

Together they gave the rocket

two coats of shiny paint.

When it was dry, Big Dog

cut a door in the rocket.

19

Next, Big Dog cut out two windows.

Now they would each have

a window to look out of.

Big Dog fetched his tool box.

He made an engine for the rocket.

(Just like that!)

Little Dog made sandwiches

while Big Dog washed his paws.

Then they filled a basket

with useful things

for the trip.

Now all they had to do was wait until the

sun went to bed and the moon got up.

Big Dog and Little Dog watched.

At last, the moon woke up.

Little Dog and Big Dog sat in the rocket
and looked out of the windows.
They looked for the moon.

The rocket leapt into the sky.

It took them lumpily, bumpily

through the night.

It shot through the clouds.

It shot past the stars.

Lumpily, bumpily it took them

to the moon.

By the time Big Dog and Little Dog arrived,

the moon had gone to sleep again.

The rocket flew round him.

Moon just blinked his black eyes

and then went back to sleep.

So Big Dog gently landed

the rocket on Moon's head.

27

Moon opened his black eyes.

Big Dog and Little Dog hopped out and

walked down to Moon's ear to speak to him.

Moon began to smile a little smile.

The smile grew bigger and bigger. . .

. . . and bigger and bigger.

Soon it was a big cheesy grin.

Big Dog and Little Dog walked

all over the moon.

Hop, bop, jump, bump they went.

Moon's cheesy grin soon turned
into a little laugh.

And a great big chuckle.

Moon was rolling around laughing.

The wispy grey clouds

under his eyes had gone.

Moon couldn't stop laughing.

So Big Dog and Little Dog

ran round the moon

while Moon grinned and giggled.

Soon Big Dog and Little Dog

were quite worn out

from so much running.

So Big Dog and Little Dog

went back to the rocket.

They ate their sandwiches

and rested their tired feet.

Big Dog and Little Dog flew home to bed.

Lumpily, bumpily through the night sky –

past the stars and through the clouds.

Gently, they landed

in their own

back garden.

Big Dog and Little Dog went straight to bed.

Soon they were fast asleep.

Moon shone down cheerfully on

Big Dog and Little Dog's house.

Big Dog and Little Dog

slept late the next morning.

When they woke up the moon had gone.

But the sun was shining.

Big Dog cooked eggs

and toast for breakfast.

Now Big Dog and Little Dog

go and visit Moon every Monday.

Moon is happy every day now . . .

. . . but he likes Mondays best.